The Deadliest Exposure

A novel by m.d head

When Tony was helping his dad one day at work, he would never have dreamed what that day would bring.It all started one Tuesday when his dad asked him to give him a hand.Tony wasn't too keen as his dad did maintenance work on the underground train.

It was long hours and filthy work, but his dad said it was a living at the end of the day.Tony still wasn't convinced though as he trudged along an on rail track that needed fixing.As his dad started working out the problem Tony glanced something twinkling in the dark tunnel.

His dad didn't need him just yet so Tony went over to the far tunnel wall.Tony thought it would end up being some piece of metal or something.As he stepped closer though it appeared to be some kind of a metal box.It was actually lodged into the tunnel wall.Tony tried dislodging it to no avail.He was determined though....

Borrowing one of his dads tools he managed to crowbar the strange object from its lodging.It was a rusty metal box, roughly the size of an average house brick.It wasn't heavy though.Tony shook it gently and heard something rattle inside.He opened the lid and saw an old fashioned looking camera with some rolls of film too.

Tony's dad suddenly gave Tony a shout."Tony, are you going to me or just mess about with rubbish all day?"Tony apologised and came back to where his dad was.He put the box in his dad's tool box and spent the rest of the day helping him.The whole time he was helping his dad though, he couldn't stop thinking about the box.

Tony took the box from his dad's tool box when they got home.His friend was into photography in a big way and even had his own red room.A room for developing camera film.Luckily for Tony his friend collected cameras as well, be they old or new.

He had them all on show in his bedroom upon shelves.Every type you could imagine, from ones used in the early 1900s to cameras that were no bigger than a matchbox as well as the modern day digital ones.Tony's knowledge of photography stopped at the average camera phone.That was good enough for him to take 'selfies' and funny pictures to text to his mates.

Once Tony got round his friends house he showed him the box."Oh yeah, you really expect me to act dumb and just open it, knowing full well it's probably booby trapped with some fail stink bomb." Peter said laughing."No mate, seriously, just take a look and tell him what you can, I'm curious as hell." Peter opened the box. precariously, knowing his friend could at times be a practical joker.

"Oh...... My......God!!!!!! Tony." Peter said."What you have in your possession is something my old history teacher told me about once."Tony was shocked and surprised at the same time.Peter went on to tell him the old teacher's tale.

'Now if I've got this right, a soldier from the 2 world war had taken up photography during the last days of the war.He wanted to take photos as a sort of memoir, good or bad.It was just his way of dealing with it I suppose.According to my old teacher, who annoyingly, past away in 2021, the soldier got into trouble with his superiors for taking photos of things he shouldn't.

He was supposed to be taking photos at a big party held by the sergeant major and various dignitaries.I think it was one of those propaganda type things. Showing the Nazis how little they had affected our troops morale and such like.This soldier had other ideas though.

As the party was drawing to a close two of the guests sneaked out and the soldier followed.He found them to be kissing and cuddling.This was obviously nothing 'out the norm' but for the fact the amorous couple consisted of a well known Nazi and a member of the Royal Family.Whats more, the female party was pregnant and placing the Nazis hand on her bump.

When the photos were later exposed they were looked over by the sergeant major.He told the would be photographer to burn the particular sensitive photos as if they were ever found they could make things particularly awkward for certain countries.The soldier assured him he would but actually kept the negatives in an old metal box along with his camera."

Peter went on to tell him that when this soldier left the army he found it hard to get a decent job.He knew though that a good photo could mean big money in the right hands.The soldier began visiting certain newspaper establishments to see if they would be interested in paying for his pics.A lot of them were either to scared or to cautious to print them though.

Eventually this guy actually did find a job as a photographer for a magazine company.One of those lifestyle,Fashion things,Who's dating who etc.While on a particular assignment he started chatting with someone who was also taking photos for 'their' magazine.The soldier thought nothing of it , just healthy competition as far as he was concerned.

The other photographer asked if the soldier was the one he heard about.The one with 'sensitive' photos.The soldier just laughed and nodded.Apparently, according to Peters teacher, that was the last time the soldier was seen alive.The next day he was found in a dark alley with a bullet hole in the back of his head.

When the police investigated the death they could find no trace of the camera he always used or the box he kept it in.After a few weeks it was old news.People were so pleased to put the terrors of war behind them, the last thing they wanted to do was read about someone shot.Peter looked hard at Tony"I could develop these for you if you want me to.I could do it now." Tony nodded."Well yeah,be interesting to see what else we might find hey."

That evening Peter and Tony were inside the 'red room' developing as much of the film as they could.They hung up all the prints on a kind of old fashioned washing line with pegs till they were dry.By the end of the evening the 'red room' was filled with developed photos,all hanging up to dry.

After another hour or so of waiting they collected all the photos that were now dry.Peter put a large stack of photos down on his bed and Tony began to look through them.There were the usual unfocused ones and those that were repeated but then......

The more Photos Tony saw the wider Peters eyes got, just like Tony's.The description sensitive photos' was something of an understatement, considering what they showed.For a short moment both the boys looked out there windows, to make sure there was nothing out the ordinary going on.Ofcourse, there wasn't but they still felt 'a bit' unsettled.

Rifling through the many photos Tony came across one that showed a former member of parliament engaged in precarious goings on with another countries counterpart and another too.The word Threesome came to mind.That wasn't all they were doing either.Among the discarded clothes were various drug related paraphernalia.

One photo was that of a prince being intimate with an attractive brunette.His brother couldn't be seen anywhere.Along with those photos there were numerous celebrities too.One showed a certain chat show host,with a speech impediment laughing while on the phone in a radio station.Tony could vaguely remember that story appearing in all the media a few years ago.

There were photos of reality stars acting quite a lot differently to how they portrayed themselves in public.This particular reality star shared his surname with a particular county.One of them was smoking something that clearly was not a normal looking cigarette for instance.

There was one photo that showed a talent show star whose surname sounded a bit like a fence who was seen being intimate with a popular page three model from yesteryear who incidentally had her own reality show .There were also a lot of photos of huge stars cheating on there partners.One of the big stars was the leader of a popular band whose wife was an actress, appearing in several comic book movies.

Some of of the photos were quite ‘grainy’ and hard to see.These were shots of various security agents from particular organisations exchanging information with other agents, during the Cold War.On closer inspection, some of the information was in those large padded envelopes you get at the post office.Sometimes the photographer had zoomed right in on the package being exchanged.You could just about see the imprint of a what looked like a weapon of some description.

After a while it became clear that whoever the person was who killed the soldier, he had a few ideas to make money that wasn't exactly ‘legit’. The next day Tony was at college studying.Knowing what his dad did for a living and just ‘how’ hard he worked he definitely wanted to do a computer based job.He had a lot of respect for his dad and loved him very much but he just knew he would never have the stamina or grit to do his dad's job every day.

He had a free hour or so before his next class so started googling.He wanted to see if he could find some info on the photos Peter and he had seen.First he tried to find who the soldier was.As hard as he searched though he just couldn't find 'anything' about him.It was almost as if all traces of the story had been wiped.Tony wasn't going to give up though.He tried typing in words like Spy Pics, Cold War photos, scandalous photos etc but it led to no avail.

Finally he tried making up words like spyfu, or scandalpic,anything that might lead him somewhere to at least start.Then, something began to happen on the screen, all the words started appearing like a pop up advert.

Like the type you get when the internet memory realises your interest in a particular thing and starts creating adverts for things the user may be interested in. This was different though, the pop ups began appearing faster and faster till suddenly small red triangles appeared in the centre on the screen.

They grew bigger and bigger till eventually hundreds upon hundreds appeared on the screen that overlapped the previous ones.
“Oh great, that’s all I need, a stupid virus “ he said to himself.Thinking nothing of it, Tony got up from his chair to call someone over.When he glanced back though he noticed the computer screen was now completely red with the words “Lock out” in large black lettering flashing on the screen.

It reminded Tony of the American movies he watched where there would be these cities with huge neon advertising boards flickering brightly.At least he could turn the TV off though or press stop on the player if they gave him a head ache.He tried turning the computer off then back on again but nothing changed apart from now there was a sort of whirring sound coming from it.Tony just collected all his stuff and decided to give college a miss that day.

As Tony left the college and waited for the bus he felt as if everyone he saw were watching him.He felt like he was in an old spy movie where eyes would follow your every move.As the bus arrived he jumped on and went u to the top deck, to sit at the back.He looked out the busses back window to see if he was still being watched.

All he saw though were men in suits going about their daily routine.Smoking outside their offices or meeting others in their lunch breaks.No, really nothin 'out the norm' at all, really.As the bus eventually pulled up at his stop Tony jumped off and walked to his house.Once inside he ran upstairs to his bedroom.The photos were in a dock draw stacked up and safe.

Tony began flicking through them again as his mobile read rung.It was Peter.He had called to ask Tony if anything unusual happened at college that day.When Tony told him about the computer debacle Peter went silent.Apparently,peters laptop did the same thing.Peter just slung it in the river though, after smashing it of course.He wasn't going to take' any' chances.Tony wondered if he should do the same.

He started flicking through the photos once more and came across a series of photos that could of been used in any spy novel.One was a man with an umbrella that was poking someone else in the side.The other was of a man who looked completely devoid of life having a syringe placed into his forearm by a man in a grey suit, while another held the poor victim still.

Another showed a very powerful Russian figure in conversation with two large looking men who Tony thought he recognised from a news article he had read last year.It was something to do with a section of the uk that had been cordoned off because an elderly gentleman and his daughter who had been found on a park bench.They had be poisoned and the area,it was believed,was also infected.

There was a very old photo of a former American president dancing at some party.This was not particularly unusual apart from the fact that he was widely thought to be wheelchair bound.There was a note on this one that said in big bold lettering 'Operation Sympathy Vote.

Another photo was taken in South Korea of a political leader,who is thought to be as mad as his father before him ,quite clearly arguing with his brother.A brother who was later found murdered.There was also a photo of a former presidents son who died in a plane crash and a former Princess who died in a crash also.There were notes on both of these that read Accident, with a question mark added.

One of the photos was more up to date.It was a former Sandy haired politician in talks with someone who organised rallies and protests and was known to various security agencies.It was dated round about the time of the Presidential elections.Tony could remember watching the news when it all happened.A bunch of thugs had invaded some building and many decent people had been injured.

Tony heard the doorbell ring and felt his heartbeat quicken slightly.He then began to feel himself perspire as he walked down stairs to get the door."Oh for goodness sake, this is stupid,"He told himself."Why would anybody be interested in a couple of college students researching old photos." He told himself,, almost trying to convince himself, once more.As he opened the door he was greeted by..........

Peter was behind the door."You will never believe what happened to me today at college." Peter said, half excited,half afraid.Tony just held his hand in front of him as if to say stop speaking."Was it anything like my day at college?" Tony said to his friend, as he went on to relate to him what had happened that day.

When Tony had finished Peter was left dumbstruck."Errrrrm,yeah,that is pretty much what happened to me."Tony invited his friend indoors and they both went upstairs to his bedroom.The photos were on Tony's bed, scattered.

"Have you got anything to drink?" Peter asked Tony."Yeah, there's some orange juice in the fridge."Peter just gave him a look."No you div,I mean alcohol." He said laughing."Oh right, I see." Tony said as he started laughing too in realisation."I didn't think you drank?" He said."Well I do 'now" Peter said looking slightly unwell.Tony went downstairs and returned with a bottle of whisky."Will this do you?" He asked his friend."He'll yeah." Came the reply as they began to giggle like little girls.

After they had both composed themselves with a few mouthfuls of whiskey they began sifting through the photos again.Amongst the pics was a photo of a man with a tattoo on his face.The boys thought it was a star but couldn't say for sure.

They spent the rest of the day sifting through the photos and gasping at what they saw.One of the photos was of a movie producer who was now in prison.He had been reported by many women for his untoward behaviour.

There was also a photo or two of someone who obviously knew a particular member of the royal family extremely well.So well in fact he was seen partying with with him and numerous young women.Tony recognised the name first,instead of the face, as the guy shared his surname with someone who helped a massive pop group in the 60's with their career.

They rifled through some more pics till they came across one that showed a popular America golfer being intimate with a number of prostitutes.Then they saw a photo of someone who used to be in a boy band in the 80s.He was seen hugging and kissing a woman who was actually married to a lead singer who fronted a huge rock band from Manchester, England.

After a week or so nothing out of the ordinary really happened.The boys did their studies at college and went about their daily routines.Tony's dad would come home from work, moaning as per usual.Usually about the way the 'real' railway staff were not being paid what they deserved.

Peter's dad was a dentist so when he came home he usually moaned about people who didn't look after their teeth as well as they should.

The next week was just the same.Except for that time some stupid driver almost ran him down, on his way from college.Tony just put it down to maybe the brakes failing.Or at least he did until he got a worrying call from Peter.

Peter had been helping his dad organise his dentistry surgery.His dad was great at his job but his organisation skills were something to be desired.A patient of his father came in for a routine check up.He was quite well to do and carried a briefcase with the letters on the front in gold leaf.As the dental assistant took his coat, she showed him to the dentist chair.

As the gentleman got into the chair he dropped something onto the floor.Within seconds Peter, his dad, the dental nurse too all collapsed to the surgery floor.Minutes later Peter felt his now heavy lids begin to open.As his eyes began to focus he could see a figure in front of him.

Peter found himself to be sitting down in, what appeared to be, a small square room with a table between him and the figure.The figure, Peter could now see, was the well to do gentlemen with the briefcase.There was a piece of A4 writing paper in front of him on the table and a simple pencil.The man told Peter that all the research him and Tony had been doing on the photos,had caught the attention of his superiors.

Portraying a very thin smile he told Peter to write down everything they had found out about the photos and where they were being kept.Peter felt his heart start to beat an inaudible pace faster than he was used to.His head began to throb as sweat began to form under his arms.

Making him feel uncomfortable whenever he moved his arm.Peter asked the guy who he worked for and if he was in trouble.The guy just said he was in no trouble yet and to continue writing.Peter just did as he was told.After,what seemed to be,ages he finally put down his pencil as the guy thanked him for his cooperation.

“So what happens now?” He asked tentatively.The man just smiled as Peter heard a hissing sound and.....,

A few moments later Peter was once again in the surgery with his father.He had the mother of all headaches and his father looked completely confused."You okay dad?"His dad answered vaguely."Yes I'm.....fine, I think, I'm sure there was a patient here just now, or Im just going mad." He said laughing.

When Tony heard all Peter had to say he started gathering all the photos together.This was 'not' what he wanted to hear.There was a knock at the door and Tony answered."Hiya, your mum called us the other day about the Satellite dish not working properly." Tony just went through the motions, "Erm, yeah, whatever". He replied to the guy as Tony watched him start getting all his equipment out of his van."Will you be long as I need to go out in a minute." He said.The guy said he would be no more than ten minutes at the most.

Once the satellite guy was busy Tony quickly raced upstairs to collect all the photos and camera together with the box it came in.He put it in his backpack and brought it downstairs while the guy finished doing whatever it was he was doing.He text Peter and said they should meet up at their usual place about 4ish.

By the time Tony had wrote and received the text messages the satellite guy was done.Tony saw him off and made his way to Peter.Once they met up they headed to Peters to go through the photos once more.One of the photos was of a former prime minister laughing and joking with members of his party,when he had previously, told the public to stay indoors to avoid spreading COVID.

Another politician was photoed enjoying a holiday when he was supposed to be back in his own country arranging help for people trying to flee a war torn country.The photo that really shocked them though was of a former princess having a part of her body sucked , while she sat in the sun.Tony and Peter both were in shock after seeing a photo of an actress, who used to be in a lifeguard tv show, frolicking with a Russian politician of considerate power and influence over many.

This photo was accompanied by one that depicted the same actress in the arms of a man who had been exiled from his own country.The boys decided that whoever the guy was who questioned Peter, it was time to cut their losses and run.Just like the subject in one of the photos.This was a huge Olympic star in the world of sport who after getting into too much trouble with various women and essentially wrecking his public image decided to transition into a woman, possibly the most famous 'Trans' in the world.

There was a very recent photo of a dance group who were popular for a short while in the UK.It was a photo showing the members of the group essentially vandalising a local church.The leader of the group who reminded Tony of a musical instrument usually appeared anywhere there was a tv camera and after a while became something of a bore.

Some photos were literally just average, everyday photos but then there were the ones that weren't.For instance there were some that showed policeman from various countries being racist and sexist to members of the public as well as there fellow police colleagues.There was one photo for instance that depicted a particular UK policeman gesturing what he planned to do to an innocent female member of the public, who later was found dead after the particular officer kidnapped, tortured, raped and murdered her.He was 'eventually' arrested and justice was dealt.

The boys decided to copy all the photos onto a usb stick that would be placed somewhere only they would know about.They put the usb stick inside a waterproof container and attached it to the underside of one of the water fountains in Trafalgar Square.

They then made there way home, looking over their shoulders all the way.They took a number of shortcuts and changed busses a few times on their way just in case they were being followed.Soon they were both home.They phoned each other once to make sure they had both made it in one piece.

As Tony said goodbye though he thought his phone sounded strange.He messaged Peter to destroy his phone as did Tony.The next day they were both at college studying.The whole day felt strange, as in the day was almost too normal a day.Each time he went from one class to the next Tony felt like everyone was watching him.Of Course they weren't but that didn't make him feel any easier.

On the way back from college the boys jumped on the bus, where they saw an old newspaper left on the back seat.Nonchalantly Peter grabbed it and started thumbing through the pages to the sport section.Hi team was playing that night and he wanted to check the time.As he started reading he heard Tony gasp."Peter, check out the front page."

As Peter did as he was asked he could now see what Tony was on about.There on the front page was an article about a man from MI5 who had been found dead in an ally."That's exactly the same thing as your old History teacher told you about that soldier, the one who originally owned the camera.Peter looked at the dead mans face and felt ill."Oh my, that's the guy who was asking questions."

When Tony got home he asked his mum about the satellite dish guy.According to his mum she had never contacted them and would of known if she did.Now Tony began to feel ill.He went upstairs and pulled a brand new pay as you go phone(non contract) out of his back pack.Tony called his friend at college who loved all things 'Tech' and asked if he could test his family's home for listening devices.Robbie the 'Tech' guy wasn't much of a sociable person and hated meeting new people too.He was however brilliant when it came to technology and anything to do with spy stuff.

His father was a massive fan of spy movies from the 40s onwards and Robbie just sort of caught the bug too.He had recently seen a device used in a film that actually detected surveillance equipment.Of Course , in the film it was disguised as something else entirely but Robbie just had to see if he could build one.Not only did he complete his task but the device he built could detect 'anything' electrical that wasn't supposed to be in a house.

As soon as he arrived at Tony's he began pulling his device from his jacket.It was no bigger than a pack of playing cards and had just two round objects on its top.One was an on/off button, the other was a small lightbulb that would light up if a foreign object was found.Robbie began upstairs, searching all the rooms and then made his way downstairs where he did the rest of the house.After about an hour or so he had found surveillance equipment throughout Tony's home.

Tony counted at least 10 listening devices found throughout the house.Some were disguised as buttons on a sofa, others took the form of a plug socket.Tony was told by Robbie that there was even one built into his computer, as well as the families landline.Robbie gave one final sweep of the house, then reassured there were no more devices,bid Tony fairly well.

Tony rang Peter to let him know Robbie would be round to check his home too.Also to discreetly check his dads dentistry surgery.Tony then made himself a sandwich and flicked on the radio.He pulled out all the photo prints from his backpack and took one last look through them before putting them all together into a large padded envelope.He made sure it was sealed tightly and wrote the address on the front,The London Transport Museum, Tony though this was kind of apt.

A few weeks later everything went back to normal and very slowly days turned into weeks that turned into months.Everyday was now normal for two college students who can often be seen grinning beside 'that' fountain at Trafalgar Square.

THE END ?

M.D Head published his first book in 2021 " Notre Dame" then went on to publish a handful of short stories including "jack casey" and his poetry books. He is now focusing on his Jack Casey adventure novels and his Chriastina novels which he is enjoying reliving the memories of playing with his nieces favourite toys and bringing them to life in this world.

www.ingramcontent.com/pod-product-compliance
Lightning Source LLC
LaVergne TN
LVHW020545160826
845677LV00015B/4219

* 9 7 9 8 3 6 6 6 8 4 1 7 0 *